Merry Christmas to You, Blue Kangaroo!

Emma Chichester Clark

A Doubleday Book for Young Readers

For Eliza

A Doubleday Book for Young Readers

Published by
Random House Children's Books
a division of
Random House, Inc.
New York

Doubleday and the anchor with dolphin colophon are registered trademarks of Random House, Inc.

Visit us on the Web! www.randomhouse.com/kids
Educators and librarians, for a variety of teaching tools, visit us at www.randomhouse.com/teachers

Library of Congress Cataloging-in-Publication data is available upon request

ISBN: 0-385-74682-2 (trade)
0-385-90918-7 (lib. bdg.)

The text of this book is set in 20-point Garamond.
MANUFACTURED IN ITALY
October 2004
10 9 8 7 6 5 4 3 2 1

Blue Kangaroo belonged to Lily.
He was her very own kangaroo,
and it was his first Christmas.
"Look!" whispered Lily. "It's snowing—
just for you, Blue Kangaroo!"

Lily made her own Christmas cards.
She drew robins and holly and she stuck stars on them.

"I've made one for everyone," she said,
"and one just for you, Blue Kangaroo!"

"Just for me!"
thought Blue Kangaroo.
"I wish I had one for Lily."

The next day, Lily and her mother made
Christmas decorations. They cut up colored
paper and stuck it with glue.

"It's going to be so pretty!" cried Lily. "And it's just for you, Blue Kangaroo!"

"And *you*," said her mother.

In the afternoon, Uncle George and Lily's father brought
the Christmas tree.
"It's Blue Kangaroo's first Christmas!" said Lily.

"Well then," said Uncle George, "here's a tree just for you,
Blue Kangaroo!"

"Just for me?"
thought Blue Kangaroo.
"What will I do with a tree?"

The next day, Lily and her mother wrapped up presents.
"I hope you're not looking, because this one's just for you,
Blue Kangaroo," said Lily.

Lily helped to put the presents under
the tree.

"Just for me!" thought Blue Kangaroo.
"I wish I had one for Lily."

Later on, Aunt Jemima and Aunt Florence came.
Aunt Jemima brought mince pies and Aunt Florence
brought gingerbread men.

"One for you, Lily, one for your little brother . . .
and this one is just for you, Blue Kangaroo!"
said Aunt Florence.

"Just for me,"
thought Blue Kangaroo.
"It's just *like* me!"

Lily's grandparents arrived in the evening.
"It's Blue Kangaroo's first Christmas!"
said Lily.

Everyone sang carols around the tree, and then Lily sang
one all by herself. "Just for you,
Blue Kangaroo!" she said.

"Just for me!"
thought Blue Kangaroo.
"I wish I could sing for Lily."

Before bed, Lily hung up her stocking.
"Do you think Father Christmas will come?" she asked.
"He'll come when you are fast asleep," said her mother.

"Good night, Blue Kangaroo," whispered Lily,
and she closed her eyes tight . . .

. . . but Blue Kangaroo
lay wide-eyed through
the night.

Suddenly, there was a funny noise.
Blue Kangaroo's whiskers bristled.
His ears tingled. "Is it Father Christmas?"
he wondered.

A big yellow moon was shining through the
house and everything was quiet.
Then he heard it again.

"It *must* be Father Christmas!" thought Blue Kangaroo.
"Perhaps he can help me."
Blue Kangaroo waited. The noises got louder . . .
then crashing, and BUMP!

"What can I do for you, Blue Kangaroo?" asked Father Christmas.
"Well, Lily says everything is just for me, but I want to give
something to her, and I haven't got anything,"
said Blue Kangaroo sadly.

"Has she been good?" asked Father Christmas.

"Oh, yes!" said Blue Kangaroo.

"Then you might find something, just right, in my sack," said Father Christmas. "Have a look."

Blue Kangaroo looked, and he found something just right.

Father Christmas wrote a label for Blue Kangaroo, so that he could hang his present on the tree. Then they had some milk and cookies.

"Good night, little kangaroo," said Father Christmas. "Lily is a lucky girl to have such a good kangaroo as you!"

In the morning, Lily ran downstairs with Blue Kangaroo.

She found that there were *three* stockings hanging on the mantelpiece!

"Look!" said Lily. "It says, 'Just for you, my good
friend, Blue Kangaroo, from Father Christmas.'
How did that happen?" she asked.

Lily began to open her stocking, but then she noticed
something else.
"Look!" she said. "A little blue heart on the Christmas tree!
That wasn't there before!"

It had a ribbon with a small label tied
onto it. Lily read it out loud. It said,

"Just for you, Lily.
Merry Christmas!
with love from
Blue Kangaroo."

Lily smiled. "And Merry Christmas
to *you*, Blue Kangaroo," she said,
hugging him tight.